HAPPY ENDING

BY
MACK REYNOLDS
AND
FREDRIC BROWN

Sometimes the queerly shaped Venusian trees seemed to talk to him, but their voices were soft. They were loyal people.

There were four men in the lifeboat that came down from the space-cruiser. Three of them were still in the uniform of the Galactic Guards.

The fourth sat in the prow of the small craft looking down at their goal, hunched and silent, bundled up in a greatcoat against the coolness of space—a greatcoat which he would never need again after this morning. The brim of his hat was pulled down far over his forehead, and he studied the nearing shore through dark-lensed glasses. Bandages, as though for a broken jaw, covered most of the lower part of his face.

He realized suddenly that the dark glasses, now that they had left the cruiser, were unnecessary. He slipped them off. After the cinematographic grays his eyes had seen through these lenses for so long, the brilliance of the color below him was almost like a blow. He blinked, and looked again.

They were rapidly settling toward a shoreline, a beach. The sand was a dazzling, unbelievable white such as had never been on his home planet. Blue the sky and water, and green the edge of the fantastic jungle. There was a flash of red in the green, as they came still closer, and he realized suddenly that it must be a *marigee*, the semi-intelligent Venusian parrot once so popular as pets throughout the solar system.

Throughout the system blood and steel had fallen from the sky and ravished the planets, but now it fell no more.

And now this. Here in this forgotten portion of an almost completely destroyed world it had not fallen at all.

Only in some place like this, alone, was safety for him. Elsewhere—anywhere—imprisonment or, more likely, death. There was danger, even here. Three of the crew of the space-cruiser knew. Perhaps, someday, one of them would talk. Then they would come for him, even here.

But that was a chance he could not avoid. Nor were the odds bad, for three people out of a whole solar system knew where he was. And those three were loyal fools.

The lifeboat came gently to rest. The hatch swung open and he stepped out and walked a few paces up the beach. He turned and waited while the two spacemen who had guided the craft brought his chest out and carried it across the beach and to the corrugated-tin shack just at the edge of the trees. That shack had once been a space-radar relay station. Now the equipment it had held was long gone, the antenna mast taken down. But the shack still stood. It would be his home for a while. A long while. The two men returned to the lifeboat preparatory to leaving.

And now the captain stood facing him, and the captain's face was a rigid mask. It seemed with an effort that the captain's right arm remained at his side, but that effort had been ordered. No salute.

The captain's voice, too, was rigid with unemotion. "Number One ..."

"Silence!" And then, less bitterly. "Come further from the boat before you again let your tongue run loose. Here." They had reached the shack.

"You are right, Number ..."

"No. I am no longer Number One. You must continue to think of me as *Mister* Smith, your cousin, whom you brought here for the reasons you explained to the under-officers, before you surrender your ship. If you *think* of me so, you will be less likely to slip in your speech."

"There is nothing further I can do—Mister Smith?"

"Nothing. Go now."

"And I am ordered to surrender the—"

"There are no orders. The war is over, lost. I would suggest thought as to what spaceport you put into. In some you may receive humane treatment. In others—"

The captain nodded. "In others, there is great hatred. Yes. That is all?"

"That is all. And, Captain, your running of the blockade, your securing of fuel *en route*, have constituted a deed of high valor. All I can give you in reward is my thanks. But now go. Goodbye."

"Not goodbye," the captain blurted impulsively, "but *hasta la vista*, *auf Wiedersehen*, *until the day* ... you will permit me, for the last time to address you and salute?"

The man in the greatcoat shrugged. "As you will."

Click of heels and a salute that once greeted the Caesars, and later the pseudo-Aryan of the 20th Century, and, but yesterday, he who was now known as *the last of the dictators*. "Farewell, Number One!"

"Farewell," he answered emotionlessly.

Mr. Smith, a black dot on the dazzling white sand, watched the lifeboat disappear up into the blue, finally into the haze of the upper atmosphere of Venus. That eternal haze that would always be there to mock his failure and his bitter solitude.

The slow days snarled by, and the sun shone dimly, and the *marigees* screamed in the early dawn and all day and at sunset, and sometimes there were the six-legged *baroons*, monkey-like in the trees, that gibbered at him. And the rains came and went away again.

At nights there were drums in the distance. Not the martial roll of marching, nor yet a threatening note of savage hate. Just drums, many miles away, throbbing rhythm for native dances or exorcising, perhaps, the forest-night demons. He assumed these Venusians had their superstitions, all other races had. There was no threat, for him, in that throbbing that was like the beating of the jungle's heart.

Mr. Smith knew that, for although his choice of destinations had been a hasty choice, yet there had been time for him to read the available reports. The natives were harmless and friendly. A Terran missionary had lived among them some time ago—before the outbreak of the war. They were a simple, weak race. They seldom went far from their villages; the space-radar operator who had once occupied the shack reported that he had never seen one of them.

So, there would be no difficulty in avoiding the natives, nor danger if he did encounter them.

Nothing to worry about, except the bitterness.

Not the bitterness of regret, but of defeat. Defeat at the hands of the defeated. The damned Martians who came back after he had driven them halfway across their damned arid planet. The Jupiter Satellite Confederation landing endlessly on the home planet, sending their vast armadas of spacecraft daily and nightly to turn his mighty cities into dust. In spite of everything; in spite of his score of ultra-vicious secret weapons and the last desperate efforts of his weakened armies, most of whose men were under twenty or over forty.

The treachery even in his own army, among his own generals and admirals. The turn of Luna, that had been the end.

His people would rise again. But not, now after Armageddon, in his lifetime. Not under him, nor another like him. The last of the dictators.

Hated by a solar system, and hating it.

It would have been intolerable, save that he was alone. He had foreseen that—the need for solitude. Alone, he was still Number One. The presence of others would have forced recognition of his miserably changed status. Alone, his pride was undamaged. His ego was intact.

The long days, and the *marigees'* screams, the slithering swish of the surf, the ghost-quiet movements of the *baroons* in the trees and the raucousness of their shrill voices. Drums.

Those sounds, and those alone. But perhaps silence would have been worse.

For the times of silence were louder. Times he would pace the beach at night and overhead would be the roar of jets and rockets, the ships that had roared over New Albuquerque, his capitol, in those last days before he had fled. The crump of bombs and the screams and the blood, and the flat voices of his folding generals.

Those were the days when the waves of hatred from the conquered peoples beat upon his country as the waves of a stormy sea beat upon crumbling cliffs. Leagues back of the battered lines, you could *feel* that hate and vengeance as a tangible thing, a thing that thickened the air, that made breathing difficult and talking futile.

And the spacecraft, the jets, the rockets, the damnable rockets, more every day and every night, and ten coming for every one shot down. Rocket ships raining hell from the sky, havoc and chaos and the end of hope.

And then he knew that he had been hearing another sound, hearing it often and long at a time. It was a voice that shouted invective and ranted hatred and glorified the steel might of his planet and the destiny of a man and a people.

It was his own voice, and it beat back the waves from the white shore, it stopped their wet encroachment upon this, his domain. It screamed back at the *baroons* and they were silent. And at times he laughed, and the *marigees* laughed. Sometimes, the queerly shaped Venusian trees talked too, but their voices were quieter. The trees were submissive, they were good subjects.

Sometimes, fantastic thoughts went through his head. The race of trees, the pure race of trees that never interbred, that stood firm always. Someday the trees—

But that was just a dream, a fancy. More real were the *marigees* and the *kifs*. They were the ones who persecuted him. There was the *marigee* who would shriek "*All is lost!*" He had shot at it a hundred times with his needle gun, but always it flew away unharmed. Sometimes it did not even fly away.

"All is lost!"

At last he wasted no more needle darts. He stalked it to strangle it with his bare hands. That was better. On what might have been the thousandth try, he caught it and killed it, and there was warm blood on his hands and feathers were flying.

That should have ended it, but it didn't. Now there were a dozen *marigees* that screamed that all was lost. Perhaps there had been a dozen all along. Now he merely shook his fist at them or threw stones.

The *kifs*, the Venusian equivalent of the Terran ant, stole his food. But that did not matter; there was plenty of food. There had been a cache of it in the shack, meant to restock a space-cruiser, and never used. The *kifs* would not get at it until he opened a can, but then, unless he ate it all at once, they ate whatever he left. That did not matter. There were plenty of cans. And always fresh fruit from the jungle. Always in season, for there were no seasons here, except the rains.

But the *kifs* served a purpose for him. They kept him sane, by giving him something tangible, something inferior, to hate.

Oh, it wasn't hatred, at first. Mere annoyance. He killed them in a routine sort of way at first. But they kept coming back. Always there were *kifs*. In his larder, wherever he did it. In his bed. He sat the legs of the cot in dishes of gasoline, but the *kifs* still got in. Perhaps they dropped from the ceiling, although he never caught them doing it.

They bothered his sleep. He'd feel them running over him, even when he'd spent an hour picking the bed clean of them by the light of the carbide lantern. They scurried with tickling little feet and he could not sleep.

He grew to hate them, and the very misery of his nights made his days more tolerable by giving them an increasing purpose. A pogrom against the *kifs*. He sought out their holes by patiently following one bearing a bit of food, and he poured gasoline into the hole and the earth around it, taking satisfaction in the thought of the writhings in agony below. He went about hunting *kifs*, to step on them. To stamp them out. He must have killed millions of *kifs*.

But always there were as many left. Never did their number seem to diminish in the slightest. Like the Martians—but unlike the Martians, they did not fight back.

Theirs was the passive resistance of a vast productivity that bred *kifs* ceaselessly, overwhelmingly, billions to replace millions. Individual *kifs* could be killed, and he took savage satisfaction in their killing, but he knew his methods were useless save for the pleasure and the purpose they gave him. Sometimes the pleasure would pall in the shadow of its futility, and he would dream of mechanized means of killing them.

He read carefully what little material there was in his tiny library about the *kif*. They were astonishingly like the ants of Terra. So much that there had been speculation about their relationship—that didn't interest him. How could they be killed, *en masse*? Once a year, for a brief period, they took on the characteristics of the army ants of Terra. They came from their holes in endless numbers and swept everything before them in their devouring march. He wet his lips when he read that. Perhaps the opportunity would come then to destroy, to destroy, *and destroy*.

Almost, Mr. Smith forgot people and the solar system and what had been. Here in this new world, there was only he and the *kifs*. The *baroons* and the *marigees* didn't count. They had no order and no system. The *kifs*—

In the intensity of his hatred there slowly filtered through a grudging admiration. The *kifs* were true totalitarians. They practiced what he had preached to a mightier race, practiced it with a thoroughness beyond the kind of man to comprehend.

Theirs the complete submergence of the individual to the state, theirs the complete ruthlessness of the true conqueror, the perfect selfless bravery of the true soldier.

But they got into his bed, into his clothes, into his food.

They crawled with intolerable tickling feet.

Nights he walked the beach, and that night was one of the noisy nights. There were high-flying, high-whining jet-craft up there in the moonlight sky and their shadows dappled the black water of the sea. The planes, the rockets, the jet-craft, they were what had ravaged his cities, had turned his railroads into twisted steel, had dropped their H-Bombs on his most vital factories.

He shook his fist at them and shrieked imprecations at the sky.

And when he had ceased shouting, there were voices on the beach. Conrad's voice in his ear, as it had sounded that day when Conrad had walked into the palace, white-faced, and forgotten the salute. "There is a breakthrough at Denver, Number One! Toronto and Monterey are in danger. And in the other hemispheres—" His voice cracked. "—the damned Martians and the traitors from Luna are driving over the Argentine. Others have landed near New Petrograd. It is a rout. All is lost!"

Voices crying, "Number One, *hail*! Number One, *hail*!"

A sea of hysterical voices. "Number One, *hail*! Number One—"

A voice that was louder, higher, more frenetic than any of the others. His memory of his own voice, calculated but inspired, as he'd heard it on play-backs of his own speeches.

The voices of children chanting, "To thee, O Number One—" He couldn't remember the rest of the words, but they had been beautiful words. That had been at the public school meet in the New Los Angeles. How strange that he should remember, here and now, the very tone of his voice and inflection, the shining wonder in their children's eyes. Children only, but they were willing to kill and die, *for him*, convinced that all that was needed to cure the ills of the race was a suitable leader to follow.

"All is lost!"

And suddenly the monster jet-craft were swooping downward and starkly he realized what a clear target he presented, here against the white moonlit beach. They must see him.

The crescendo of motors as he ran, sobbing now in fear, for the cover of the jungle. Into the screening shadow of the giant trees, and the sheltering blackness.

He stumbled and fell, was up and running again. And now his eyes could see in the dimmer moonlight that filtered through the branches overhead. Stirrings there, in the branches. Stirrings and voices in the night. Voices in and of the night. Whispers and shrieks of pain. Yes, he'd shown them pain, and now their tortured voices ran with him through the knee-deep, night-wet grass among the trees.

The night was hideous with noise. Red noises, an almost *tangible* din that he could nearly *feel* as well as he could see and hear it. And after a while his breath came raspingly, and there was a thumping sound that was the beating of his heart and the beating of the night.

And then, he could run no longer, and he clutched a tree to keep from falling, his arms trembling about it, and his face pressed against the impersonal roughness of the bark. There was no wind, but the tree swayed back and forth and his body with it.

Then, as abruptly as light goes on when a switch is thrown, the noise vanished. Utter silence, and at last he was strong enough to let go his grip on the tree and stand erect again, to look about to get his bearings.

One tree was like another, and for a moment he thought he'd have to stay here until daylight. Then he remembered that the sound of the surf would give him his directions. He listened hard and heard it, faint and far away.

And another sound—one that he had never heard before—faint, also, but seeming to come from his right and quite near.

He looked that way, and there was a patch of opening in the trees above. The grass was waving strangely in that area of moonlight. It moved, although there was no breeze to move it. And there was an almost sudden *edge*, beyond which the blades thinned out quickly to barrenness.

And the sound—it was like the sound of the surf, but it was continuous. It was more like the rustle of dry leaves, but there were no dry leaves to rustle.

Mr. Smith took a step toward the sound and looked down. More grass bent, and fell, and vanished, even as he looked. Beyond the moving edge of devastation was a brown floor of the moving bodies of *kifs*.

Row after row, orderly rank after orderly rank, marching resistlessly onward. Billions of *kifs*, an army of *kifs*, eating their way across the night.

Fascinated, he stared down at them. There was no danger, for their progress was slow. He retreated a step to keep beyond their front rank. The sound, then, was the sound of chewing.

He could see one edge of the column, and it was a neat, orderly edge. And there was discipline, for the ones on the outside were larger than those in the center.

He retreated another step—and then, quite suddenly, his body was afire in several spreading places. The vanguard. Ahead of the rank that ate away the grass.

His boots were brown with *kifs*.

Screaming with pain, he whirled about and ran, beating with his hands at the burning spots on his body. He ran head-on into a tree, bruising his face horribly, and the night was scarlet with pain and shooting fire.

But he staggered on, almost blindly, running, writhing, tearing off his clothes as he ran.

This, then, was *pain*. There was a shrill screaming in his ears that must have been the sound of his own voice.

When he could no longer run, he crawled. Naked, now, and with only a few *kifs* still clinging to him. And the blind tangent of his flight had taken him well out of the path of the advancing army.

But stark fear and the memory of unendurable pain drove him on. His knees raw now, he could no longer crawl. But he got himself erect again on trembling legs, and staggered on. Catching hold of a tree and pushing himself away from it to catch the next.

Falling, rising, falling again. His throat raw from the screaming invective of his hate. Bushes and the rough bark of trees tore his flesh.

Into the village compound just before dawn, staggered a man, a naked terrestrial. He looked about with dull eyes that seemed to see nothing and understand nothing.

The females and young ran before him, even the males retreated.

He stood there, swaying, and the incredulous eyes of the natives widened as they saw the condition of his body, and the blankness of his eyes.

When he made no hostile move, they came closer again, formed a wondering, chattering circle about him, these Venusian humanoids. Some ran to bring the chief and the chief's son, who knew everything.

The mad, naked human opened his lips as though he were going to speak, but instead, he fell. He fell, as a dead man falls. But when they turned him over in the dust, they saw that his chest still rose and fell in labored breathing.

And then came Alwa, the aged chieftain, and Nrana, his son. Alwa gave quick, excited orders. Two of the men carried Mr. Smith into the chief's hut, and the wives of the chief and the chief's son took over the Earthling's care, and rubbed him with a soothing and healing salve.

But for days and nights he lay without moving and without speaking or opening his eyes, and they did not know whether he would live or die.

Then, at last, he opened his eyes. And he talked, although they could make out nothing of the things he said.

Nrana came and listened, for Nrana of all of them spoke and understood best the Earthling's language, for he had been the special protege of the Terran missionary who had lived with them for a while.

Nrana listened, but he shook his head. "The words," he said, "the words are of the Terran tongue, but I make nothing of them. His mind is not well."

The aged Alwa said, "Aie. Stay beside him. Perhaps as his body heals, his words will be beautiful words as were the words of the Father-of-Us who, in the Terran tongue, taught us of the gods and their good."

So they cared for him well, and his wounds healed, and the day came when he opened his eyes and saw the handsome blue-complexioned face of Nrana sitting there beside him, and Nrana said softly, "Good day, Mr. Man of Earth. You feel better, no?"

There was no answer, and the deep-sunken eyes of the man on the sleeping mat stared, glared at him. Nrana could see that those eyes were not yet sane, but he saw, too, that the madness in them was not the same that it had been. Nrana did not know the words for delirium and paranoia, but he could distinguish between them.

No longer was the Earthling a raving maniac, and Nrana made a very common error, an error more civilized beings than he have often made. He thought the paranoia was an improvement over the wider madness. He talked on, hoping the Earthling would talk too, and he did not recognize the danger of his silence.

"We welcome you, Earthling," he said, "and hope that you will live among us, as did the Father-of-Us, Mr. Gerhardt. He taught us to worship the true gods of the high heavens. Jehovah, and Jesus and their prophets the men from the skies. He taught us to pray and to love our enemies."

And Nrana shook his head sadly, "But many of our tribe have gone back to the older gods, the cruel gods. They say there has been great strife among the outsiders, and no more remain upon all of Venus. My father, Alwa, and I are glad another one has come. You will be able to help those of us who have gone back. You can teach us love and kindliness."

The eyes of the dictator closed. Nrana did not know whether or not he slept, but Nrana stood up quietly to leave the hut. In the doorway, he turned and said, "We pray for you."

And then, joyously, he ran out of the village to seek the others, who were gathering bela-berries for the feast of the fourth event.

When, with several of them, he returned to the village, the Earthling was gone. The hut was empty.

Outside the compound they found, at last, the trail of his passing. They followed and it led to a stream and along the stream until they came to the tabu of the green pool, and could go no farther.

"He went downstream," said Alwa gravely. "He sought the sea and the beach. He was well then, in his mind, for he knew that all streams go to the sea."

"Perhaps he had a ship-of-the-sky there at the beach," Nrana said worriedly. "All Earthlings come from the sky. The Father-of-Us told us that."

"Perhaps he will come back to us," said Alwa. His old eyes misted.

Mr. Smith was coming back all right, and sooner than they had dared to hope. As soon in fact, as he could make the trip to the shack and return. He came back dressed in clothing very different from the garb the other white man had worn. Shining leather boots and the uniform of the Galactic Guard, and a wide leather belt with a holster for his needle gun.

But the gun was in his hand when, at dusk, he strode into the compound.

He said, "I am Number One, the Lord of all the Solar System, and your ruler. Who was chief among you?"

Alwa had been in his hut, but he heard the words and came out. He understood the words, but not their meaning. He said, "Earthling, we welcome you back. I am the chief."

"You were the chief. Now you will serve me. I am the chief."

Alwa's old eyes were bewildered at the strangeness of this. He said, "I will serve you, yes. All of us. But it is not fitting that an Earthling should be chief among—"

The whisper of the needle gun. Alwa's wrinkled hands went to his scrawny neck where, just off the center, was a sudden tiny pin prick of a hole. A faint trickle of red coursed over the dark blue of his skin. The old man's knees gave way under him as the rage of the poisoned needle dart struck him, and he fell. Others started toward him.

"Back," said Mr. Smith. "Let him die slowly that you may all see what happens to—"

But one of the chief's wives, one who did not understand the speech of Earth, was already lifting Alwa's head. The needle gun whispered again, and she fell forward across him.

"I am Number One," said Mr. Smith, "and Lord of all the planets. All who oppose me, die by—"

And then, suddenly all of them were running toward him. His finger pressed the trigger and four of them died before the avalanche of their bodies bore him down and overwhelmed him. Nrana had been first in that rush, and Nrana died.

The others tied the Earthling up and threw him into one of the huts. And then, while the women began wailing for the dead, the men made council.

They elected Kallana chief and he stood before them and said, "The Father-of-Us, the Mister Gerhardt, deceived us." There was fear and worry in his voice and apprehension on his blue face. "If this be indeed the Lord of whom he told us—"

"He is not a god," said another. "He is an Earthling, but there have been such before on Venus, many many of them who came long and long ago from the skies. Now they are all dead, killed in strife among themselves. It is well. This last one is one of them, but he is mad."

And they talked long and the dusk grew into night while they talked of what they must do. The gleam of firelight upon their bodies, and the waiting drummer.

The problem was difficult. To harm one who was mad was tabu. If he was really a god, it would be worse. Thunder and lightning from the sky would destroy the village. Yet they dared not release him. Even if they took the evil weapon-that-whispered-its-death and buried it, he might find other ways to harm them. He might have another where he had gone for the first.

Yes, it was a difficult problem for them, but the eldest and wisest of them, one M'Ganne, gave them at last the answer.

"O Kallana," he said, "Let us give him to the *kifs*. If *they* harm him—" and old M'Ganne grinned a toothless, mirthless grin "—it would be their doing and not ours."

Kallana shuddered. "It is the most horrible of all deaths. And if he is a god—"

"If he is a god, they will not harm him. If he is mad and not a god, we will not have harmed him. It harms not a man to tie him to a tree."

Kallana considered well, for the safety of his people was at stake. Considering, he remembered how Alwa and Nrana had died.

He said, "It is right."

The waiting drummer began the rhythm of the council-end, and those of the men who were young and fleet lighted torches in the fire and went out into the forest to seek the *kifs*, who were still in their season of marching.

And after a while, having found what they sought, they returned.

They took the Earthling out with them, then, and tied him to a tree. They left him there, and they left the gag over his lips because they did not wish to hear his screams when the *kifs* came.

The cloth of the gag would be eaten, too, but by that time, there would be no flesh under it from which a scream might come.

They left him, and went back to the compound, and the drums took up the rhythm of propitiation to the gods for what they had done. For they had, they knew, cut very close to the corner of a tabu—but the provocation had been great and they hoped they would not be punished.

All night the drums would throb.

The man tied to the tree struggled with his bonds, but they were strong and his writhings made the knots but tighten.

His eyes became accustomed to the darkness.

He tried to shout, "I am Number One, Lord of—"

And then, because he could not shout and because he could not loosen himself, there came a rift in his madness. He remembered who he was, and all the old hatreds and bitterness welled up in him.

He remembered, too, what had happened in the compound, and wondered why the Venusian natives had not killed him. Why, instead, they had tied him here alone in the darkness of the jungle.

Afar, he heard the throbbing of the drums, and they were like the beating of the heart of night, and there was a louder, nearer sound that was the pulse of blood in his ears as the fear came to him.

The fear that he knew why they had tied him here. The horrible, gibbering fear that, for the last time, an army marched against him.

He had time to savor that fear to the uttermost, to have it become a creeping certainty that crawled into the black corners of his soul as would the soldiers of the coming army crawl into his ears and nostrils while others would eat away his eyelids to get at the eyes behind them.

And then, and only then, did he hear the sound that was like the rustle of dry leaves, in a dank, black jungle where there were no dry leaves to rustle nor breeze to rustle them.

Horribly, Number One, the last of the dictators, did not go mad again; not exactly, but he laughed, and laughed and laughed....

EARTHMEN BEARING GIFTS

BY
FREDRIC BROWN

Mars had gifts to offer and Earth had much in return—if delivery could be arranged!

DHAR Ry sat alone in his room, meditating. From outside the door he caught a thought wave equivalent to a knock, and, glancing at the door, he willed it to slide open.

It opened. "Enter, my friend," he said. He could have projected the idea telepathically; but with only two persons present, speech was more polite.

Ejon Khee entered. "You are up late tonight, my leader," he said.

"Yes, Khee. Within an hour the Earth rocket is due to land, and I wish to see it. Yes, I know, it will [p149] land a thousand miles away, if their calculations are correct. Beyond the horizon. But if it lands even twice that far the flash of the atomic explosion should be visible. And I have waited long for first contact. For even though no Earthman will be on that rocket, it will still be first contact—for them. Of course our telepath teams have been reading their thoughts for many centuries, but—this will be the first *physical* contact between Mars and Earth."

Khee made himself comfortable on one of the low chairs. "True," he said. "I have not followed recent reports too closely, though. Why are they using an atomic warhead? I know they suppose our planet is uninhabited, but still—"

"They will watch the flash through their lunar telescopes and get a—what do they call it?—a spectroscopic analysis. That will tell them more than they know now (or think they know; much of it is erroneous) about the atmosphere of our planet and the composition of its surface. It is—call it a sighting shot, Khee. They'll be here in person within a few oppositions. And then—"

Mars was holding out, waiting for Earth to come. What was left of Mars, that is; this one small city of about nine hundred beings. The civilization of Mars was older than that of Earth, but it was a dying one. This was what remained of it: one city, nine hundred people.

They were waiting for Earth to make contact, for a selfish reason and for an unselfish one.

MARTIAN civilization had developed in a quite different direction from that of Earth. It had developed no important knowledge of the physical sciences, no technology. But it had developed social sciences to the point where there had not been a single crime, let alone a war, on Mars for fifty thousand years. And it had developed fully the parapsychological sciences of the mind, which Earth was just beginning to discover.

Mars could teach Earth much. How to avoid crime and war to begin with. Beyond those simple things lay telepathy, telekinesis, empathy….

And Earth would, Mars hoped, teach them something even more valuable to Mars: how, by science and technology—which it was too late for Mars to develop now, even if they had the type of minds which would enable them to develop these things—to restore and rehabilitate a dying planet, so that an otherwise dying race might live and multiply again.

Each planet would gain greatly, and neither would lose.

And tonight was the night when Earth would make its first sighting shot. Its next shot, a rocket containing Earthmen, or at least an Earthman, would be at the next opposition, two Earth years, or roughly four Martian years, hence. The Martians knew this, because their teams of telepaths were able to catch at least some of the thoughts of Earthmen, enough to know their plans. Unfortunately, at that distance, the connection was one-way. Mars could not ask Earth to hurry its program. Or tell Earth scientists the facts about Mars' composition and atmosphere which would have made this preliminary shot unnecessary.

Tonight Ry, the leader (as nearly as the Martian word can be translated), and Khee, his administrative assistant and closest friend, sat and meditated together until the time was near. Then they drank a toast to the future—in a beverage based on menthol, which had the same effect on Martians as alcohol on Earthmen—and climbed to the roof of the building in which they had been sitting. They watched toward the north, where the rocket should land. The stars shone brilliantly and unwinkingly through the atmosphere.

IN Observatory No. 1 on Earth's moon, Rog Everett, his eye at the eyepiece of the spotter scope, said triumphantly, "Thar she blew,

Willie. And now, as soon as the films are developed, we'll know the score on that old planet Mars." He straightened up—there'd be no more to see now—and he and Willie Sanger shook hands solemnly. It was an historical occasion.

"Hope it didn't kill anybody. Any Martians, that is. Rog, did it hit dead center in Syrtis Major?"

"Near as matters. I'd say it was maybe a thousand miles off, to the south. And that's damn close on a fifty-million-mile shot. Willie, do you really think there are any Martians?"

Willie thought a second and then said, "No."

He was right.

Hall of Mirrors

BY
FREDRIC BROWN

It is a tough decision to make—whether to give up your life so you can live it over again!

For an instant you think it is temporary blindness, this sudden dark that comes in the middle of a bright afternoon.

It *must* be blindness, you think; could the sun that was tanning you have gone out instantaneously, leaving you in utter blackness?

Then the nerves of your body tell you that you are *standing*, whereas only a second ago you were sitting comfortably, almost reclining, in a canvas chair. In the patio of a friend's house in Beverly Hills. Talking to Barbara, your fiancée. Looking at Barbara—Barbara in a swim suit—her skin golden tan in the brilliant sunshine, beautiful.

You wore swimming trunks. Now you do not feel them on you; the slight pressure of the elastic waistband is no longer there against your waist. You touch your hands to your hips. You are naked. And standing.

Whatever has happened to you is more than a change to sudden darkness or to sudden blindness.

You raise your hands gropingly before you. They touch a plain smooth surface, a wall. You spread them apart and each hand reaches a corner. You pivot slowly. A second wall, then a third, then a door. You are in a closet about four feet square.

Your hand finds the knob of the door. It turns and you push the door open.

There is light now. The door has opened to a lighted room ... a room that you have never seen before.

It is not large, but it is pleasantly furnished—although the furniture is of a style that is strange to you. Modesty makes you open the door cautiously the rest of the way. But the room is empty of people.

You step into the room, turning to look behind you into the closet, which is now illuminated by light from the room. The closet is and is not a closet; it is the size and shape of one, but it contains nothing, not a single hook, no rod for hanging clothes, no shelf. It is an empty, blank-walled, four-by-four-foot space.

You close the door to it and stand looking around the room. It is about twelve by sixteen feet. There is one door, but it is closed. There are no windows. Five pieces of furniture. Four of them you recognize—more or less. One looks like a very functional desk. One is obviously a chair ... a comfortable-looking one. There is a table, although its top is on several levels instead of only one. Another is a bed, or couch. Something shimmering is lying across it and you walk over and pick the shimmering something up and examine it. It is a garment.

You are naked, so you put it on. Slippers are part way under the bed (or couch) and you slide your feet into them. They fit, and they feel warm and comfortable as nothing you have ever worn on your feet has felt. Like lamb's wool, but softer.

You are dressed now. You look at the door—the only door of the room except that of the closet (closet?) from which you entered it. You walk to the door and before you try the knob, you see the small typewritten sign pasted just above it that reads:

This door has a time lock set to open in one hour. For reasons you will soon understand, it is better that you do not leave this room before then. There is a letter for you on the desk. Please read it.

It is not signed. You look at the desk and see that there is an envelope lying on it.

You do not yet go to take that envelope from the desk and read the letter that must be in it.

Why not? Because you are frightened.

You see other things about the room. The lighting has no source that you can discover. It comes from nowhere. It is not indirect lighting; the ceiling and the walls are not reflecting it at all.

They didn't have lighting like that, back where you came from. What did you mean by *back where you came from*?

You close your eyes. You tell yourself: I am Norman Hastings. I am an associate professor of mathematics at the University of Southern California. I am twenty-five years old, and this is the year nineteen hundred and fifty-four.

You open your eyes and look again.

They didn't use that style of furniture in Los Angeles—or anywhere else that you know of—in 1954. That thing over in the corner—

you can't even guess what it is. So might your grandfather, at your age, have looked at a television set.

You look down at yourself, at the shimmering garment that you found waiting for you. With thumb and forefinger you feel its texture.

It's like nothing you've ever touched before.

I am Norman Hastings. This is nineteen hundred and fifty-four.

Suddenly you must know, and at once.

You go to the desk and pick up the envelope that lies upon it. Your name is typed on the outside: *Norman Hastings.*

Your hands shake a little as you open it. Do you blame them?

There are several pages, typewritten. Dear Norman, it starts. You turn quickly to the end to look for the signature. It is unsigned.

You turn back and start reading.

"Do not be afraid. There is nothing to fear, but much to explain. Much that you must understand before the time lock opens that door. Much that you must accept and—obey.

"You have already guessed that you are in the future—in what, to you, seems to be the future. The clothes and the room must have told you that. I planned it that way so the shock would not be too sudden, so you would realize it over the course of several minutes rather than read it here—and quite probably disbelieve what you read.

"The 'closet' from which you have just stepped is, as you have by now realized, a time machine. From it you stepped into the world of 2004. The date is April 7th, just fifty years from the time you last remember.

"You cannot return.

"I did this to you and you may hate me for it; I do not know. That is up to you to decide, but it does not matter. What does matter, and not to you alone, is another decision which you must make. I am incapable of making it.

"Who is writing this to you? I would rather not tell you just yet. By the time you have finished reading this, even though it is not signed (for I knew you would look first for a signature), I will not need to tell you who I am. You will know.

"I am seventy-five years of age. I have, in this year 2004, been studying 'time' for thirty of those years. I have completed the first time machine ever built—and thus far, its construction, even the fact that it has been constructed, is my own secret.

"You have just participated in the first major experiment. It will be your responsibility to decide whether there shall ever be any more experiments with it, whether it should be given to the world, or whether it should be destroyed and never used again."

End of the first page. You look up for a moment, hesitating to turn the next page. Already you suspect what is coming.

You turn the page.

"I constructed the first time machine a week ago. My calculations had told me that it would work, but not how it would work. I had expected it to send an object back in time—it works backward in time only, not forward—physically unchanged and intact.

"My first experiment showed me my error. I placed a cube of metal in the machine—it was a miniature of the one you just walked out of—and set the machine to go backward ten years. I flicked the switch and opened the door, expecting to find the cube vanished. Instead I found it had crumbled to powder.

"I put in another cube and sent it two years back. The second cube came back unchanged, except that it was newer, shinier.

"That gave me the answer. I had been expecting the cubes to go back in time, and they had done so, but not in the sense I had expected them to. Those metal cubes had been fabricated about three years previously. I had sent the first one back years before it had existed in its fabricated form. Ten years ago it had been ore. The machine returned it to that state.

"Do you see how our previous theories of time travel have been wrong? We expected to be able to step into a time machine in, say, 2004, set it for fifty years back, and then step out in the year 1954 ... but it does not work that way. The machine does not move in time. Only whatever is within the machine is affected, and then just with relation to itself and not to the rest of the Universe.

"I confirmed this with guinea pigs by sending one six weeks old five weeks back and it came out a baby.

"I need not outline all my experiments here. You will find a record of them in the desk and you can study it later.

"Do you understand now what has happened to you, Norman?"

You begin to understand. And you begin to sweat.

The *I* who wrote that letter you are now reading is *you*, yourself at the age of seventy-five, in this year of 2004. You are that seventy-five-year-old man, with your body returned to what it had been fifty years ago, with all the memories of fifty years of living wiped out.

You invented the time machine.

And before you used it on yourself, you made these arrangements to help you orient yourself. You wrote yourself the letter which you are now reading.

But if those fifty years are—to you—gone, what of all your friends, those you loved? What of your parents? What of the girl you are going—were going—to marry?

You read on:

"Yes, you will want to know what has happened. Mom died in 1963, Dad in 1968. You married Barbara in 1956. I am sorry to tell you that she died only three years later, in a plane crash. You have one son. He is still living; his name is Walter; he is now forty-six years old and is an accountant in Kansas City."

Tears come into your eyes and for a moment you can no longer read. Barbara dead—dead for forty-five years. And only minutes ago, in subjective time, you were sitting next to her, sitting in the bright sun in a Beverly Hills patio ...

You force yourself to read again.

"But back to the discovery. You begin to see some of its implications. You will need time to think to see all of them.

"It does not permit time travel as we have thought of time travel, but it gives us immortality of a sort. Immortality of the kind I have temporarily given us.

"*Is it good?* Is it worth while to lose the memory of fifty years of one's life in order to return one's body to relative youth? The only way I can find out is to try, as soon as I have finished writing this and made my other preparations.

"You will know the answer.

"But before you decide, remember that there is another problem, more important than the psychological one. I mean overpopulation.

"If our discovery is given to the world, if all who are old or dying can make themselves young again, the population will almost double every generation. Nor would the world—not even our own relatively enlightened country—be willing to accept compulsory birth control as a solution.

"Give this to the world, as the world is today in 2004, and within a generation there will be famine, suffering, war. Perhaps a complete collapse of civilization.

"Yes, we have reached other planets, but they are not suitable for colonizing. The stars may be our answer, but we are a long way from reaching them. When we do, someday, the billions of habitable planets that must be out there will be our answer ... our living room. But until then, what is the answer?

"Destroy the machine? But think of the countless lives it can save, the suffering it can prevent. Think of what it would mean to a man dying of cancer. Think ..."

Think. You finish the letter and put it down.

You think of Barbara dead for forty-five years. And of the fact that you were married to her for three years and that those years are lost to you.

Fifty years lost. You damn the old man of seventy-five whom you became and who has done this to you ... who has given you this decision to make.

Bitterly, you know what the decision must be. You think that *he* knew, too, and realize that he could safely leave it in your hands. Damn him, he *should* have known.

Too valuable to destroy, too dangerous to give.

The other answer is painfully obvious.

You must be custodian of this discovery and keep it secret until it is safe to give, until mankind has expanded to the stars and has new worlds to populate, or until, even without that, he has reached a state of civilization where he can avoid overpopulation by rationing births to the number of accidental—or voluntary—deaths.

If neither of those things has happened in another fifty years (and are they likely so soon?), then you, at seventy-five, will be writing another letter like this one. You will be undergoing another experience similar to the one you're going through now. And making the same decision, of course.

Why not? You'll be the same person again.

Time and again, to preserve this secret until Man is ready for it.

How often will you again sit at a desk like this one, thinking the thoughts you are thinking now, feeling the grief you now feel?

There is a click at the door and you know that the time lock has opened, that you are now free to leave this room, free to start a new life for yourself in place of the one you have already lived and lost.

But you are in no hurry now to walk directly through that door.

You sit there, staring straight ahead of you blindly, seeing in your mind's eye the vista of a set of facing mirrors, like those in an old-fashioned barber shop, reflecting the same thing over and over again, diminishing into far distance.

Keep Out

BY
Fredric Brown

With no more room left on Earth, and with Mars hanging up there empty of life, somebody hit on the plan of starting a colony on the Red Planet. It meant changing the habits and physical structure of the immigrants, but that worked out fine. In fact, every possible factor was covered—except one of the flaws of human nature....

Daptine is the secret of it. Adaptine, they called it first; then it got shortened to daptine. It let us adapt.

They explained it all to us when we were ten years old; I guess they thought we were too young to understand before then, although we knew a lot of it already. They told us just after we landed on Mars.

"You're *home*, children," the Head Teacher told us after we had gone into the glassite dome they'd built for us there. And he told us there'd be a special lecture for us that evening, an important one that we must all attend.

And that evening he told us the whole story and the whys and wherefores. He stood up before us. He had to wear a heated space suit and helmet, of course, because the temperature in the dome was comfortable for us but already freezing cold for him and the air was already too thin for him to breathe. His voice came to us by radio from inside his helmet.

"Children," he said, "you are home. This is Mars, the planet on which you will spend the rest of your lives. You are Martians, the first Martians. You have lived five years on Earth and another five in space. Now you will spend ten years, until you are adults, in this dome, although toward the end of that time you will be allowed to spend increasingly long periods outdoors.

"Then you will go forth and make your own homes, live your own lives, as Martians. You will intermarry and your children will breed true. They too will be Martians.

"It is time you were told the history of this great experiment of which each of you is a part."

Then he told us.

Man, he said, had first reached Mars in 1985. It had been uninhabited by intelligent life (there is plenty of plant life and a few varieties of non-flying insects) and he had found it by terrestrial standards uninhabitable. Man could survive on Mars only by living inside glassite domes and wearing space suits when he went outside of them. Except by day in the warmer seasons it was too cold for him. The air was too thin for him to breathe and long exposure to sunlight—less filtered of rays harmful to him than on Earth because of the lesser atmosphere—could kill him. The plants were chemically alien to him and he could not eat them; he had to bring all his food from Earth or grow it in hydroponic tanks.

For fifty years he had tried to colonize Mars and all his efforts had failed. Besides this dome which had been built for us there was only one other outpost, another glassite dome much smaller and less than a mile away.

It had looked as though mankind could never spread to the other planets of the solar system besides Earth for of all of them Mars was the least inhospitable; if he couldn't live here there was no use even trying to colonize the others.

And then, in 2034, thirty years ago, a brilliant biochemist named Waymoth had discovered daptine. A miracle drug that worked not on the animal or person to whom it was given, but on the progeny he conceived during a limited period of time after inoculation.

It gave his progeny almost limitless adaptability to changing conditions, provided the changes were made gradually.

Dr. Waymoth had inoculated and then mated a pair of guinea pigs; they had borne a litter of five and by placing each member of the litter under different and gradually changing conditions, he had obtained amazing results. When they attained maturity one of those guinea pigs was living comfortably at a temperature of forty below zero Fahrenheit, another was quite happy at a hundred and fifty above. A third was thriving on a diet that would have been deadly poison for an ordinary animal and a fourth was contented under a constant X-ray bombardment that would have killed one of its parents within minutes.

Subsequent experiments with many litters showed that animals who had been adapted to similar conditions bred true and their progeny was conditioned from birth to live under those conditions.

"Ten years later, ten years ago," the Head Teacher told us, "you children were born. Born of parents carefully selected from those who volunteered for the experiment. And from birth you have been brought up under carefully controlled and gradually changing conditions.

"From the time you were born the air you have breathed has been very gradually thinned and its oxygen content reduced. Your lungs have compensated by becoming much greater in capacity, which is why your chests are so much larger than those of your teachers and attendants; when you are fully mature and are breathing air like that of Mars, the difference will be even greater.

"Your bodies are growing fur to enable you to stand the increasing cold. You are comfortable now under conditions which would kill ordinary people quickly. Since you were four years old your nurses and teachers have had to wear special protection to survive conditions that seem normal to you.

"In another ten years, at maturity, you will be completely acclimated to Mars. Its air will be your air; its food plants your food. Its extremes of temperature will be easy for you to endure and its median temperatures pleasant to you. Already, because of the five years we spent in space under gradually decreased gravitational pull, the gravity of Mars seems normal to you.

"It will be your planet, to live on and to populate. You are the children of Earth but you are the first Martians."

Of course we had known a lot of those things already.

The last year was the best. By then the air inside the dome—except for the pressurized parts where our teachers and attendants live—was almost like that outside, and we were allowed out for increasingly long periods. It is good to be in the open.

The last few months they relaxed segregation of the sexes so we could begin choosing mates, although they told us there is to be no marriage until after the final day, after our full clearance. Choosing was not difficult in my case. I had made my choice long since and I'd felt sure that she felt the same way; I was right.

Tomorrow is the day of our freedom. Tomorrow we will be Martians, *the* Martians. Tomorrow we shall take over the planet.

Some among us are impatient, have been impatient for weeks now, but wiser counsel prevailed and we are waiting. We have waited twenty years and we can wait until the final day.

And tomorrow is the final day.

Tomorrow, at a signal, we will kill the teachers and the other Earthmen among us before we go forth. They do not suspect, so it will be easy.

We have dissimulated for years now, and they do not know how we hate them. They do not know how disgusting and hideous we find them, with their ugly misshapen bodies, so narrow-shouldered and tiny-chested, their weak sibilant voices that need amplification to carry in our Martian air, and above all their white pasty hairless skins.

We shall kill them and then we shall go and smash the other dome so all the Earthmen there will die too.

If more Earthmen ever come to punish us, we can live and hide in the hills where they'll never find us. And if they try to build more domes here we'll smash them. We want no more to do with Earth.

This is our planet and we want no aliens. Keep off!

Two Timer

By
Fredric Brown

Here is a brace of vignettes by the Old Vignette Master ... short and sharp ... like a hypodermic!

Experiment

"The first time machine, gentlemen," Professor Johnson proudly informed his two colleagues. "True, it is a small-scale experimental model. It will operate only on objects weighing less than three pounds, five ounces and for distances into the past and future of twelve minutes or less. But it works."

The small-scale model looked like a small scale—a postage scale—except for two dials in the part under the platform.

Professor Johnson held up a small metal cube. "Our experimental object," he said, "is a brass cube weighing one pound, two point three ounces. First, I shall send it five minutes into the future."

He leaned forward and set one of the dials on the time machine. "Look at your watches," he said.

They looked at their watches. Professor Johnson placed the cube gently on the machine's platform. It vanished.

Five minutes later, to the second, it reappeared.

Professor Johnson picked it up. "Now five minutes into the past." He set the other dial. Holding the cube in his hand he looked at his watch. "It is six minutes before three o'clock. I shall now activate the mechanism—by placing the cube on the platform—at exactly three o'clock. Therefore, the cube should, at five minutes before three, vanish from my hand and appear on the platform, five minutes before I place it there."

"How can you place it there, then?" asked one of his colleagues.

"It will, as my hand approaches, vanish from the platform and appear in my hand to be placed there. Three o'clock. Notice, please."

The cube vanished from his hand.

It appeared on the platform of the time machine.

"See? Five minutes before I shall place it there, it *is* there!"

His other colleague frowned at the cube. "But," he said, "what if, now that it has already appeared five minutes before you place it there, you should change your mind about doing so and *not* place it there at three o'clock? Wouldn't there be a paradox of some sort involved?"

"An interesting idea," Professor Johnson said. "I had not thought of it, and it will be interesting to try. Very well, I shall *not* ..."

There was no paradox at all. The cube remained.

But the entire rest of the Universe, professors and all, vanished.

Sentry

He was wet and muddy and hungry and cold, and he was fifty thousand light-years from home.

A strange blue sun gave light and the gravity, twice what he was used to, made every movement difficult.

But in tens of thousands of years this part of war hadn't changed. The flyboys were fine with their sleek spaceships and their fancy weapons. When the chips are down, though, it was still the foot soldier, the infantry, that had to take the ground and hold it, foot by bloody foot. Like this damned planet of a star he'd never heard of until they'd landed him there. And now it was sacred ground because the aliens were there too. *The* aliens, the only other intelligent race in the Galaxy ... cruel, hideous and repulsive monsters.

Contact had been made with them near the center of the Galaxy, after the slow, difficult colonization of a dozen thousand planets; and it had been war at sight; they'd shot without even trying to negotiate, or to make peace.

Now, planet by bitter planet, it was being fought out.

He was wet and muddy and hungry and cold, and the day was raw with a high wind that hurt his eyes. But the aliens were trying to infiltrate and every sentry post was vital.

He stayed alert, gun ready. Fifty thousand light-years from home, fighting on a strange world and wondering if he'd ever live to see home again.

And then he saw one of them crawling toward him. He drew a bead and fired. The alien made that strange horrible sound they all make, then lay still.

He shuddered at the sound and sight of the alien lying there. One ought to be able to get used to them after a while, but he'd never been able to. Such repulsive creatures they were, with only two arms and two legs, ghastly white skins and no scales.

You may also enjoy ...

Wandering Between Two Worlds: Essays on Faith and Art
Anita Mathias
Benediction Books, 2007
152 pages
ISBN: 0955373700

Available from www.amazon.com, www.amazon.co.uk
www.wanderingbetweentwoworlds.com

In these wide-ranging lyrical essays, Anita Mathias writes, in lush, lovely prose, of her naughty Catholic childhood in Jamshedpur, India; her large, eccentric family in Mangalore, a sea-coast town converted by the Portuguese in the sixteenth century; her rebellion and atheism as a teenager in her Himalayan boarding school, run by German missionary nuns, St. Mary's Convent, Nainital; and her abrupt religious conversion after which she entered Mother Teresa's convent in Calcutta as a novice. Later rich, elegant essays explore the dualities of her life as a writer, mother, and Christian in the United States--Domesticity and Art, Writing and Prayer, and the experience of being "an alien and stranger" as an immigrant in America, sensing the need for roots.

About the Author

Anita Mathias was born in India, has a B.A. and M.A. in English from Somerville College, Oxford University and an M.A. in Creative Writing from the Ohio State University. Her essays have been published in The Washington Post, The London Magazine, The Virginia Quarterly Review, Commonweal, Notre Dame Magazine, America, The Christian Century, Religion Online, The Southwest Review, Contemporary Literary Criticism, New Letters, The Journal, and two of HarperSanFrancisco's The Best Spiritual Writing anthologies. Her non-fiction has won fellowships from The National Endowment for the Arts; The Minnesota State Arts Board; The Jerome Foundation, The Vermont Studio Center; The Virginia Centre for the Creative Arts, and the First Prize for the Best General Interest Article from the Catholic Press Association of the United States and Canada. Anita has taught Creative Writing at the College of William and Mary, and now lives and writes in Oxford, England.
Website: www.anitamathias.com/
Blog: wanderingbetweentwoworlds.blogspot.com/

www.ingramcontent.com/pod-product-compliance
Ingram Content Group UK Ltd.
Pitfield, Milton Keynes, MK11 3LW, UK
UKHW041833200726
13854UKWH00003BA/1113